BEYOND THE CRACK IN THE SIDEWALK

MARYANN MILLER

To my daughter, Cindy, who loves stories as much as I do.

A NOTE FROM THE AUTHOR

I've written short stories off and on most of my life, and three of those included in this collection were written some years ago; others more recently. Most of the stories explore some aspect of living and loving and dying, which to me are three elements that define our human existence in many ways. One story, *Over the Threshold*, doesn't quite fit that mold and was written when my muse suggested something along the lines of a "Twilight Zone" story. In *Going Back*, a father and son try to reconcile a fractured relationship, as do a mother and daughter in *A Coming Of Age*. The title story, *Beyond the Crack in the Sidewalk*, looks at homelessness from the eyes of young teens. I hope you enjoy meeting these very different characters and getting a glimpse into their disparate lives. When you finish reading, it would be a great honor if you would leave a quick review on Amazon.

Thank you,

Maryann

CONTENTS

GOING BACK

WITH A LOW, steady rumble, the last train of the night rolled out of the station and lumbered down the track. Now the station was deserted except for the lone man who stood smoking a cigarette and staring at the train as the lights from passenger cars slipped into the darkness. Mike was always amazed that the short two-hour train ride from Dallas could be so much like stepping back into time. Any minute he expected a bunch of outlaws to come tearing out of the night on lathered horses and stop the train before it rolled out of sight. The setting was very much Old West, and he even remembered when a movie company had filmed a train robbery right there in the early sixties.

That had been an eternity ago.

Now it was April 14, 1970, and Mike O'Leary was fresh out of Vietnam. He was far removed from the excited, young kid who'd watched the filming of that western. And he was far removed from the boy who'd listened to his dad talk about his home-coming from the Big One. That's the way he always talked about World War II, "The Big One."

"That was the one that made every man a hero," his dad would say, slapping him on the back with a great amount of bravado. "Boy, I can still remember the cheering crowds as the troop ship docked. And the ticker tape parade. And all the excitement. All those people cheering and waving to show how much they appreciated what we did for them."

Mike had always liked to hear those stories, but that's all they were to him. Stories. They weren't any more real than the adventure books he used to read, and he hadn't thought about them in years. Until his own homecoming.

There were no parades. No cheering crowds. Not even a friendly face as he got off the plane at L.A. International. People took one look at his uni-form and turned away. Some in disgust and some in simple dismissal, much like some people do when they look at a child. No one greeted him, or shook his hand, or said one kind word to him as he made his way halfway across the world to come home.

He wanted to shout at them, "Look at me! Talk

to me! Make me believe that all those lives weren't wasted over there in that jungle. Make me believe in something, anything ... myself."

But he didn't shout. He just continued his solitary trip home, an angry, bitter, disillusioned man who couldn't make up his mind about where to direct his anger.

Should he be angry at the ironic twist of fate that had always kept him from measuring up to his father? That same ironic twist of fate that had made his war one that lacked all the clarity of purpose his father's war had enjoyed. Or should he be disillusioned with the people who set up the standards by which men were measured? Or with himself because he still found it so difficult to stand up for the man he was, still trying so hard to be the man his father had always wanted him to be?

Or should he be bitter about the stroke of luck that had brought him through eighteen months of combat unscathed, while all around him good, decent men left their lives and their blood on that battlefield? Perhaps the guys who died over there were the lucky ones after all. There were no survivors from war. Just men who came home in a uniform instead of a green plastic bag.

Mike knew his father would be proud of his war record and the medals in black boxes, hidden away in his duffle. Two pieces of silver that stood in mute testimony to his courage and manhood. But would his father understand the reality of the gut-wrenching fear and the trembling uncertainty that denied that manhood?

Or perhaps he should be bitter about his relationship with John that had sustained him through it all, revealing a part of himself that Mike had carefully denied from the day he was fifteen?

As Mike stood there breathing deeply of the cool, clean air, he knew almost instinctively that the thin shred of relationship that bound them together, father and son, hung in the balance of this homecoming.

He ground out his cigarette on the creaky, old planks of the platform, hoisted his duffle bag over his broad shoulders, and headed for the station house. As he drew near, he recognized the battered pickup parked in front. It was the same pile of rusty, dented metal that had carried him and his friends around the cow town of Comanche for years. Then Mike made out the figure of a man casually leaning against the side of the truck. There was no mistaking the man either. Even in the darkness, Mike recognized the powerful presence of Tom O'Leary.

The older man, clad in Levi's, Stetson, and boots rose to his full and impressive six-feet four as he watched his son approaching. For a minute, he wasn't sure it was Mike. He'd changed, grown taller and added some muscle. And Tom wondered what horrors had caused the harsh lines on Mike's face. Or was it more than that? Was it that something intangible that had troubled him for as long as he could remember? Tom's friends had always respectfully ignored Mike's lack of enthusiasm for 'manly endeavors', but Tom knew what they'd been thinking. With this homecoming, Mike could prove himself once and for all, and Tom knew he had just as much at stake as Mike did.

"Mike ... Mike ... it's so good to have you home," Tom said. "You'll never know how much we worried about you. How are you?"

Mike shook his father's calloused hand. "I'm fine, Dad. Just fine."

Tom looked at his son for a long time. The dark circles under Mike's eyes and the hollowness of his cheeks didn't escape his shrewd scrutiny. "Are you really? You look awfully tired and thin."

"I'll be all right with a little bit of rest and some good food."

"Then we'd best be going. Toss your gear in the back and climb aboard."

The two men bounced along the rutted gravel road in silence. Mike sensed that his father was just as uncomfortable as he was, and he hesitated to encroach upon the older man's privacy.

"Well," his father finally said, his rough voice

cracking the silence like a whip. "Some of the boys thought we could have a barbecue tomorrow night. Sort of celebrate your homecoming, and give you a chance to tell us all about it."

"That's nice, Dad, but I don't think I'm ready for that."

"Sure. If you're too tired, we could make it another night."

Mike hesitated a moment then said, "It's not that. I just don't want to talk about it yet."

The dismissal in Mike's voice made Tom curb his next response and drive on in silence.

As they passed the outbuildings of the Lazy L Ranch and neared the main house, Tom saw it all with pride, and a sense of belonging filled every fiber of his being. It was like coming home from church and putting on his boots and jeans. There was something proper and fitting and comfortable about the ranch, and it was the only place Tom ever felt completely at home. His only regret was that his wife, Mattie, gone now for ten years, hadn't lived to enjoy it with him.

Mike saw it all as if he were a stranger just visiting.

The house was just as he remembered; tall and stately, resembling the huge mansions that graced southern plantations, and he was touched by the peaceful beauty of it all. But he never thought of it as his, that it belonged to him or he to it. Not the way his father did. The only place that gave Mike a sense of belonging was on the range working the cattle. The other things considered manly left him feeling like an outsider.

Tom turned off the engine. The only sound to be heard was the night wind rustling through the cottonwoods that were just beginning to leaf out. It was a peaceful scene, and neither of the men seemed to be in any hurry to go into the house. They sat there in the silence for a few moments and then Tom turned to Mike. "If you don't want to have a barbecue at all, we don't have to. You're calling the shots."

Mike glanced quickly at his father. "Am I, Dad? Am I really?"

"Of course. You're a man now, and you earned the right to be your own boss. I understand what you've been through, and if you want a few days—"

"It's more than that," Mike said. "Not just the war."

Again, there was a harshness in Mike's voice that seemed to be warning Tom off, but this time he spoke up, "What do you mean?"

"The differences. The conflicts. The barriers that have always stood between us."

Tom shook his head. "I never wanted it that

way," he said, his voice hard. "I tried to make things work between us."

"Some things aren't as easy to manipulate as others," Mike said, careful to keep his voice from rising. "You can't control life the way you do this ranch."

Tom shot his son an angry look. "Do we have to start an argument on your first night home?"

Mike sighed. "I don't want to argue, Dad. I never did in the past either. But it's time we understand each other. The only way we can do that is to talk to each other. No anger. No shouting. Just talking."

Tom seemed to ponder Mike's words for a few minutes, then he got out of the truck and walked around the yard with his hands thrust deep in the pockets of his jeans.

After a moment, Mike got out and went over. "We could at least go in and have a drink."

"Sure, Son." Tom turned to Mike with obvious relief. "You must be awful tired after all that traveling."

Tom smiled, but Mike noticed his father's eyes were still troubled. He touched the older man lightly on the shoulder, then grabbed his bag out of the truck and headed inside. He took his things to his room on the second floor. It was still the same as when he'd left a little over three years ago, and the sameness made him smile.

After a stop in the bathroom, Mike went back downstairs and joined his father in the den. The large, comfortable room held heavy, rich leather furniture, and hunting trophies were mounted above the stone fireplace. Definitely a man's room, from the well-stocked bar to the oak gun cabinet in the corner with enough weapons in it to outfit a good-sized posse, if there were such things anymore.

Mike sat down in one of the chairs in front of the fireplace, and Tom came over to hand him a glass with a generous amount of straight bourbon. "Here's to your safe return." Tom raised his glass and took a hefty swallow. Then he set the glass down on the table, sat down opposite Mike, and took a cigar out of the humidor.

"Nothing in the world like good Kentucky bourbon and a fine cigar." Tom snipped the end of the cigar and tasted it. He pushed the box toward Mike. "You want one?"

"No thanks, I'll stick with cigarettes." Mike shifted in his seat, wishing he could feel more comfortable in the room, but he'd never liked it here. Everything was too large and too overpowering, but it seemed to suit his father. As the man had fixed the drinks and prepared his cigar it was as if the very essence of the room seeped into him and made him a whole person.

Tom's voice startled Mike out of his contemplation. "You have any plans now?"

"Nothing definite. Like to help out around here for a while. Decide after that what I want to do."

"We sure could use an extra hand right now." Tom rose and took their glasses over to the bar for a refill. "Gonna be bringing the calves in for branding."

"Knew it was about time. That's why I thought I'd stick around for a while."

"To be honest, I been hoping you'd stick around a lot longer than a while."

"I know," Mike said, accepting the glass from his father. "But this might not be where I belong—"

"Hell! There's no question of belonging. This ranch is just as much yours as it is mine."

Mike looked away without a response.

Seconds ticked away in an uneasy silence, then Tom asked, "Then what is it that you want to do?"

"I really don't know." Mike sighed and glanced back at his father. "I just need time to sort out everything that's happened."

"I don't mean to push you, but—"

"Then don't push me, Dad, please." The grimness was back on Mike's face, and the sharp edge in his tone told Tom to back off.

"Okay," Tom said with an effort at joviality. "I won't push anymore. We can talk about it later. Whenever you're ready. Right now, let's just be thankful you're home."

Tom raised his glass in salute, and the two men finished their drinks. Then Mike stood and carried his empty glass over to the bar. "I'm bushed. Think I'll go to bed."

For several weeks Mike literally tried to lose himself in work. He rode right along with the hired hands on the spring round-ups and did more than his share of the branding. This was the part of ranch life that Mike had always enjoyed—the work. There was nothing better than to be out in the open with the sun beating down on him and the strong animal smell of horses and cows permeating the air. He liked the feel of a good horse working with him as a single unit, cutting and roping, and the gentle breeze that dried the sweat that gathered on both of them. And he liked how his body responded to his demands. He didn't even mind the stiffness and soreness in his muscles at the end of the day. That was somehow very satisfying. He'd often thought that if he could just be a hired hand, he might feel very much at home here.

As just another cowboy, he wouldn't have to try so hard to forget that one basic flaw that separated him from all the other men. He could just drift from place to place. No one would have to know. And if the truth was discovered, it wouldn't matter, he could just move on. But now, he didn't want to move on. He wanted to stay. Find a way to make things work.

Mike wished his mother was still alive. Something deep inside told him that she would've understood, and she'd been the only person in the world with enough influence to force his father to be reasonable about some things. But she was gone, and there was no sense in wishing. If wishing meant anything, he could simply wish it all away.

One evening as he sat outside alone, listening to the wind sighing through a stand of pines and catching an occasional howl from a far-off coyote, Mike realized that he had to stop thinking about what to do and just do it. Tell his father and hope for the best. Over the past few weeks, he'd begun to feel an affinity with the ranch he'd never experienced before, and he thought for the first time in his life that he could stay here long term. If only his father could accept him.

Several days later, Mike looked through the open door of his father's den and saw him sitting at the massive oak desk, making precise entries in a ledger book.

"Dad," Mike said as he took a couple of tentative steps into the room. "You busy?"

"Never too busy." Tom closed the ledger and walked over to the bar. "Care for a drink?"

"Sure. Bourbon."

Tom mixed the drinks, handed a glass to Mike and sat down. "We're having a good year. Numbers are way up."

"Glad to hear it." Mike raised his glass in salute.

The men sat there in silence for a few minutes, sipping the amber liquid, then Tom asked, "What's on your mind?"

"You asked about my plans before. So now I'd like to tell you."

"Okay, let's have it."

Mike took a big swallow of his drink, then said, "I want to stay here at the ranch."

"Well, Son, that makes me mighty happy."

"I know I've made things rough for you before. Always talking like I wanted to leave for good. But now I know there's no other place I'd rather be. Even though I'll never be the kind of rancher you are."

Tom raised his glass in a salute. "That'll come in time, Mike."

"No, Dad. It won't. We're two different people. It's about time we both accepted that." Mike swirled the amber liquid in his glass. "I've learned something about myself in the past three years." He paused and took a breath, then continued. "I can't expect you to understand or accept it. I'm still having a hard time with it myself."

Mike hesitated again, and silence hung over the room like heavy clouds before a storm. Tom went over to the bar and poured another drink, some of the liquid sloshing over the rim. Watching, Mike saw that his father's composure was slipping. His hands trembled as he raised the glass to his lips. He just stood there, as if he was holding himself away from what Mike might say. Did he already know?

Mike almost lost his nerve. Maybe it would be better unsaid. Could he stand to see that tower of pride crumble before his eyes? Would either one of them be a whole person afterwards? He felt the rage building in him as it had a thousand times before. He wanted it all to go away. To become a nightmare he could wake up from. Then he wouldn't have to suffer this agony or inflict it on anyone else.

"God!" Mike threw his glass against the fireplace where it crashed into a million pieces, shards of glass skittering across the large gray stones of the hearth.

Tom turned and walked over to stand in front of Mike. "What is so awful you can't say it?"

Mike returned his father's level gaze, and thought that this might be the last time his father would ever look at him with any kind of pride. It was a full minute before he could speak. Without dropping his eyes, he said, "Dad, I'm never going to be like you. I can't be like you ... I'm gay."

Mike's voice had been barely a whisper, but Tom heard the words thundering around in his head like a stampeding herd of cattle. He wanted to scream and yell and lash out against the very words that had been spoken. Nausea crawled up this throat, and for a brief instant, he thought he might puke. It couldn't be true. This was his son ... flesh of his flesh ... he couldn't be a ... a ...

Tom found it impossible to say the word. It revolted him. He couldn't stand the painful look in Mike's eyes, so he turned away. The last time he'd seen that kind of pain, he'd shot the poor coyote that had been trying to escape the steel jaws of the trap that held him captive.

"I didn't want it to be this way," Mike said in a stilted voice that slowly penetrated the fog of misery shrouding Tom's consciousness. "I'd do anything to change. Go back in time and emerge the son you always wanted. But I can't. God knows I've tried. And I'll understand if you want me to just go away."

Mike turned and started walking toward the door.

"Wait."

Mike stopped, but he didn't turn around.

"I don't know what to say." Tom's voice was choked with emotion. "I can't believe it. I don't want to believe it."

"I don't want to, either," Mike said quietly. "I always keep hoping ... and sometimes I don't like myself very much. But still ... there it is."

Tom stared at the ramrod stiffness of his son's back, and he realized with a sudden anguish that there stood his only link with the past or the future. He went over and put a tentative hand on Mike's shoulder. He could feel Mike's muscles tense beneath the fabric of his shirt, as he held himself in rigid control. "Just give me some time," Tom said.

Mike nodded, still not turning around to face his father. "I'll go up to the old hunting cabin for a while. Give us both time."

Tom didn't respond.

"I'll pack a horse and be gone in the morning." Mike walked out of the room without looking back.

Tom stood, unable to get his shaking legs to move. His insides were empty, and a wave of loneliness washed over him, more intense than when Mattie had died. He could remember every minute, every second of that horrible day, and he never thought he could feel any more anguish than that.

"Oh, Mattie," he said softly. "What am I going to do?" He tried to imagine how she would react if she were there. What would she say?

After staggering to his chair and slumping into it, he realized what she would say. "This is our son, and nothing can change that."

He heard the words clearly in his mind. Daring him, even challenging him.

Tom walked over to the bar, mixed another drink, and took it over to the chair in front of the fireplace. The fire had almost died out, but a small flame still flickered with life. It reflected on the broken glass littering the stone hearth, the shards glittering like early morning dew.

He was mildly surprised that he saw it that way. He was never much for poetic thoughts. Being a man of action, he left the intellectual stuff to men of books and higher learning. But there seemed to be some significance here. Something his mind was trying to tell him. To help him understand that he had a choice. To leave the relationship broken, or try to put it back together. Could he find the courage to love his son and still be revolted by his homosexuality?

There. He'd said it. My son is a homosexual. He could almost see Mattie smiling down at him.

He put his drink on the table, turned out the light, and walked up the darkened stairway. Halfway down the hall, he stopped at Mike's room, where the door was slightly ajar. He could see his son in the shafts of pale moonlight that filtered through the window. Mike was sleeping fitfully, and as Tom watched him toss around, he was reminded of the little boy who used to dream of ghosts and goblins. The little boy who would run to his father to be comforted, believing that Tom could chase the ghosts away.

Tom knew that the same little boy was still inside Mike, and Tom wished with all his heart that he could chase away the ghost that haunted his son now. The ghost that would haunt them both for a long time. But he knew he couldn't do that. He couldn't take this trouble away from either of them. Somehow, they had to learn to live with it. They might spend a lifetime trying, and they might not succeed, but at least they had to try. And the first step for Tom was right there for him to take.

NO TIME TO DIE

"OH, ME … OH, DEAR GOD … OH … " The eerie, ghostlike moans filled the room, yet I wasn't sure where they came from. To halt the tumble of cloudy thoughts, I made my body go still, and the sing-song stopped. Where was it coming from?

My mind struggled for clarity, but it kept swaying, slithering into delirium like a snake going into the darkness of its hole. I know. I'm imagining it. No. There it is again.

"Oh, dear … no … no … " The words echoed and re-echoed in the darkness.

I opened my eyes and reality crept softly in. The end was near, but it hadn't happened yet. The knifing pain in my chest reminded me that I was still alive. Waiting. There was joy in the pain, but also a sad disappointment. It would be better to have the thing done with.

Then a cloud of fear swept over me like a smothering wave, and I rang for the nurse.

I did not want to be alone with that fear.

———

"Damn," Nancy muttered as the moaning increased in volume. "Why doesn't she shut up?"

Swallowing her impatience, Nancy slipped out of bed and padded across the hard, tile floor to the other side of the room. It was the first time she'd found the courage to approach since being admitted. She'd told herself it was out of respect for the woman's privacy, but she knew better.

Now, the urgent tone of the old lady's voice drew her like a siren.

Sadness took her heart in a painful grip as Nancy looked at the frail, skeleton of a person who barely made a mound under the blanket. Except for the faint rise and fall of a delicate chest, the woman could be dead, and for Nancy, it was too much like seeing her grandmother lying so still in a coffin two years ago. "Damn you," she whispered to ears that did not hear. "Damn you for making me remember."

Wanting to escape the past and the present,

Nancy turned away, then stopped when the old woman moved her hand. The motion was a light flutter, like a butterfly taking flight, and Nancy couldn't resist the impulse to reach out.

"Emily? Is that you?"

The hoarse voice split the silence, the sound startling Nancy as much as the words. Who the hell was Emily?

Another whisper of sound distracted her, and Nancy turned to see a nurse step around the door. The middle-aged woman regarded Nancy with weariness pinching her face. "What are you doing out of bed?"

"I couldn't sleep," Nancy replied, moving out of the nurse's way. "I got up to see if there was anything I could do."

"Your doctor ordered bed rest for you." The nurse snapped on latex gloves then inserted the needle of a syringe into the old woman's IV port. "Let us handle the other patients."

After the door closed behind the nurse, the room settled into quiet darkness again.

———

"Please don't leave me ... please don't leave me!" There it was again. That terrible moaning. I opened my eyes and tried to determine where the sound came from, but nothing was discernible in the lights and shadows floating around the room. Everything seemed to be suspended in time, like objects thrown randomly into the outer reaches of space.

"Why am I not dead yet? I'm ready."

Did I say that?

I don't know.

Maybe.

Then with my next breath, the fog cleared and I was acutely aware of the pain again. A pain that brought reality into sharp focus: the opaque light fixture on the ceiling, the empty chair across the room, the tube that dripped life into my arm, the faint hiss of the oxygen that reminded my lungs to breathe.

I felt the pain cut deep, like it was using a scalpel to reach the core of my being. In a moment the pain would be unbearable. Then I'd have to ring for the needle, which would mercifully bring relief.

Unmercifully, it would also put me back into non-existence.

———

Sounds of distress filled the room, waking Nancy again. Realizing the noise came from the old woman; Nancy threw back the covers and raced to the other bed. Pain seemed to pull at the woman, tossing her frail body from side to side. Nancy held on to frail shoulders, trying to still the thrashing and fighting a terrible fear that some brittle bone would break in her hands. But she couldn't ignore the distress, could she?

Nancy whirled when she heard the door open again, accompanied by the soft pats of approaching footsteps. Her heart thumped so hard she thought it might burst out of her chest as she stepped aside, braced for the scolding that didn't come. The nurse quietly did an instant replay, medicating the woman then waiting a few minutes for the sedative to calm the agitation, then she left.

A soft sigh drew Nancy's attention back to the bed. She knew she really should go back to sleep, but a conflict of emotions held her immobile until pity won out. Gently taking the old woman's hand, Nancy smoothed the dry wrinkles on skin as delicate as fine old lace. It was a moment not unlike one of the last she'd shared with her grandmother, and it brought another wave of sadness. But it wasn't just for her loss. Some of it was for the present, and she stayed until the old woman was deeply asleep.

The next morning, Nancy awoke to blessed silence and an appointment with radiology. She welcomed the time away from the old woman and the constant awareness of her situation. It wasn't any of her business, right? She should just ignore it. That's what her head told her. But her heart kept reminding her that it was unconscionable for that woman to be here in this place alone.

When the x-ray session ended, Nancy was more than ready to spend a few hours in bed. She was tired of being pushed, probed, dyed, and sloshed around a cold, steel table. She also welcomed the opportunity to stay in her room so she could satisfy her curiosity about Emily. If she was that important to the old lady, surely she'd show up sometime that day.

Afternoon dragged into early evening, and still the mysterious Emily failed to make an appearance. Nancy had dozed some, but she was sure she wouldn't have missed the disruption of someone entering the room.

When the nurse came in for rounds, Nancy decided to ask about the old woman's family, specifically Emily.

"We don't discuss patient's business." The nurse shot her a withering look.

"Well, she keeps calling out for her. And last night she thought I was this Emily person." Nancy returned the glare with defiance. "It might be nice to know who I'm supposed to be if we have another little chat tonight."

"All right." Clipped tones betrayed reluctance. "Emily is her daughter."

"Oh." Nancy paused to digest that information. "Doesn't she come to visit?"

"Not often."

"Oh." Nancy paused again. "She must live pretty far away."

"No. But she's ... well, she's busy. And that's all I'm going to say." The nurse clamped her lips tightly closed as if an undisciplined word might slip through a crack, then she hurried out the door.

Moved by a sudden rush of compassion, Nancy got up and went over to the other bed. That poor old lady, so alone and so pitiful. It seemed like the most natural thing to do, to reach out and touch the woman's hand again.

"Emily? Emily? Is that you?"

The words were framed in a raspy whisper, and tears welled in Nancy's eyes. This is ridiculous, she thought, but her voice defied her good sense. "Yes. I'm here."

Heaviness became an ache in Nancy's stomach as she held the small hand. She didn't have to be a medical expert to recognize that the old lady was dying, and she couldn't imagine it happening in a more ungraceful way. This body, only a day or two from the morgue and trussed up with all these tubes and hoses, was barely encouraging each new heartbeat. What was it like to lay there hour after hour in semi-consciousness, waiting for the last breath to come and wondering why it hadn't yet? Or did the old lady even know or care?

Just pull all the tubes. That's all it would take. It wouldn't be like killing someone. She's already dead; her body just hasn't caught up with the concept.

"No!" Nancy jerked herself away from the unwelcome thought and hurried back to the sanctuary of her own bed. How could she even think such a thing?

Nancy punched a crater in the middle of her pillow and settled in, but sleep didn't come easily. Her mind whirled with the endless circle of questions, and the constant reminders from the other side of the room pulled at her.

The old woman's pain was like another entity that had taken up residence. It was so real, Nancy was sure she could reach out and touch it. The constant buzz and click of the IV machine played like the soundtrack of a film waiting for a bit of dialogue to satisfy the audience, but the incoherent ramblings from the old woman that rose and fell like birds playing in the wind, didn't offer clarity of the story.

Hours later, Nancy fell into a restless sleep only to be jolted awake by a terrifying nightmare. She touched her sweat-drenched face to assure herself that she wasn't really that old woman who had been hunted by faceless people trying to exterminate her.

In her dream world she'd run wildly down a dark alley, but ghostly creatures had kept up with her, gaining as her stride faltered. Oh, God! They were catching her. She stumbled. Fell. Felt the cold cement against her cheek. Saw a wave of darkness coming for her. "Help me. Help me," she cried in her daze, and the cry echoed in the dark hospital room.

"Help me! Help me!"

Nancy realized the cry was no longer hers alone. Jumping up, she crossed to the other bed and looked at the old woman, surprised to see clarity in the faded blue eyes gazing back at her.

"Who are you?"

Nancy didn't know how to respond. Prepared to play the part of Emily again, she wasn't sure she could handle the real thing. "Uh, my name is Nancy. I'm, uh, in the other bed."

The old lady reached out and grabbed Nancy's hand in a surprisingly strong grip. "Please, Nancy," she pleaded. "You've got to help me."

"Well, I, uh ... I don't know what I can do." Nancy pulled away from the force of desperation clutching at her.

"Please." The voice crackled like stiff cellophane. "I want to die. Please let me die!"

Then the old woman's moment of reality folded up like an evening flower and she slipped back into unconsciousness.

At first, Nancy wasn't sure she'd actually heard the words. Maybe she just wanted to think she had. But in her heart, she knew.

God, what am I supposed to do?

Distress stirred the old woman, flailing thin, bruised arms against the railing, and Nancy's heart thudded in her chest.

Ignoring the possible consequences if the nurse should come in, Nancy sat on the edge of the bed and gathered the old woman in her arms.

It was like holding air.

"Emily? Oh, Emily, you came."

Nancy lightly touched a tear that had squeezed out of the old woman's eye. "Yes. It's okay now."

Guided by an ancient instinct imprinted in DNA by the first woman who'd ever cradled a dying mother, Nancy gently rocked the old woman, murmuring a symphony of soothing words. She could feel the sting of her own tears and found them somehow fitting.

TO LOVE AGAIN

FIRST PUBLISHED IN THE ANTHOLOGY
SHORT & HAPPY BY S&H PUBLISHING

GLORIA HURRIED into the Starbucks and saw her friend already seated with a latte. She waved, then headed to the bar for coffee. Or maybe she should have tea. Something soothing. Her nerves had been all a jangle ever since the visit from Frederick the evening before. She couldn't wait to tell her friend why he'd come.

She ordered a chamomile tea, and when it was ready, she took the cup and joined Felicia. Early that morning, Gloria had called and asked Felicia to meet her at the coffee shop, tantalizing her by saying she had the most amazing news to share. Felicia had pleaded for Gloria to tell her straight away, but Gloria put her off, telling her it had to be said face to face.

Now her friend looked over at her, excitement flashing in her eyes. "Okay, now are you going to tell me?"

"This man I know from Sunday school came to visit me last evening."

"Okay."

"Frederick. His name is Frederick."

"Okay." The look on Felicia's face clearly indicated she found nothing so amazing about this. "So? What did this Frederick have to say?"

"'I've come to *court* you, Gloria.'"

Felicia stifled a laugh. "Really? That's what he said? Nobody talks like that nowadays."

"That's what I told him."

"What? Your response was to correct him?"

Gloria sighed. "I didn't correct him. I merely pointed out that people don't court these days. According to my grandson, people hook up."

"I've heard that, too. Not exactly sure I know what that means."

"Me either. But maybe we're better off not knowing."

Felicia took a sip of her coffee, then asked, "Okay. What did you tell him?"

"I told him I didn't know. I'd have to think about it."

"Well, don't think too long. We're not teenagers

anymore. We're not even fifty-somethings anymore."

Gloria stirred more sugar into her tea. "What would you do?"

"Don't put it off on me." Felicia laughed. "This is a decision you have to make."

When Gloria didn't respond, Felicia went to the counter to buy a couple of blueberry scones. She brought them back and slid one over to her friend. "So, tell me. How do you feel about this man wanting to *court* you?"

"I'm not sure." Gloria broke open the scone and buttered half. "I like him. He and his late wife were good friends, so I know what kind of a man he is. He was so good to her when she was sick."

"He sounds like a terrific guy."

"Yes. He is. But we're old. Well past the stage of falling in love."

"Gloria Keith, I can't believe you said that. You who always lives life to the fullest."

"This is different."

Gloria averted her eyes, making a big production out of buttering the second half of her pastry, and Felicia said, "You're scared, aren't you."

It was a statement, not a question. Gloria recognized that, but she still felt a need to explain. "Wouldn't you be? Ray was the only man I've ever loved. The only one I have ever been with. You know, hooked up. What if Frederick wants to ... you know?"

Felicia laughed. "It's only an evening out. And if he was so formal as to say he wants to court you, I doubt he'll ask you to go to bed on the first date."

"Don't be crass."

Sometimes Felicia could be a little rough around the edges, but that had always further endeared her to Gloria. She'd been taught that ladies don't say bad words or talk in public about what went on between a man and a woman, and Felicia's openness was sometimes like a breath of fresh air. Despite their differences, they'd developed a bond deep enough that allowed Felica to be crass and Gloria to be prim without diminishing the friendship.

"I've got an idea," Gloria said, wiping bits of butter off her fingers with a napkin. "Why don't you and Dave join us for a dinner? I could cook and invite Frederick over and that way it wouldn't be like a real date."

"But what if he wants a real date?" Felicia grinned. "What if he wants to kiss you good night at the end of the evening?"

Gloria's neck grew warm at the thought. And much to her chagrin, so did another part of her anatomy. "You're being crass again."

"No, I'm not. Just think about it for a minute. It's

clear he has some expectations. You just have to decide if you have any."

Gloria folded her napkin into smaller and smaller squares. "I just thought that part of life was over. After Ray ... you know. I'm almost seventy for Pete's sake."

"Does that mean you just sit in your rocking chair on the back porch and let the rest of your life just blow on by?"

Gloria tried to find an answer, but words failed her.

"That's not the Gloria I know," Felicia said. "My friend Gloria has never been afraid to jump into a new adventure."

All the way home, Gloria thought about what Felicia had said. *Is it true? Am I just too scared to entertain the idea of a new adventure?*

She pulled her little Honda into the detached garage, then walked to her back door. Instead of passing the rocking chair on the rear porch, she paused, thinking she might sit down for a moment. But then again, maybe not. She ran her hand along the back, giving it a gentle push. As the chair slowly rocked back and forth, Gloria wiped her sweating palms on her slacks and walked into the house.

If she didn't call Frederick right now, she might never do it.

A COMING OF AGE

JENNY JOINED her husband on the front porch and relaxed against the back of the swing while breathing a sigh of relief. The baby was finally asleep, and the other two kids were in bed. Whether they were asleep or not, Jenny didn't know. Nor did she care.

"Tired?" Michael asked.

"Yeah. It's been one of those days." Concealed beneath her standard reply, Jenny felt a need to tell him more. She wanted to describe how she felt that afternoon when the baby was screaming, the phone was ringing, the soup was spilling over the top of the saucepan, and Danny and Matthew were destroying the living room playing war games. But trying to verbalize it made it all seem so petty, so much like a scene contrived on Medicine Avenue to sell bath oil.

How could she explain the way all that nonsense was making her feel when she didn't understand it herself?

She, Jenny Corbett, had chosen motherhood and domesticity and was a great advocate of her right to so choose. So why wasn't she content? On one level she knew, but she didn't fully *get* why the lot she'd chosen for her life was this great dichotomy between happy Mommy moments and being so overwhelmed she wanted to chuck it all. If she didn't understand, how could she expect Michael to? How could she tell him about that great knot of fear twisting itself around inside her each time she realized how easily her own frustration could turn her into an instant replay of her mother. Not that her mother had been horrible in the role. She didn't abuse her or her sister. She was just always so remote, just going through the motions, and never taking time to do more than cook supper and wash clothes. Being a mother entailed so much more, and an emotional commitment she'd never found in her own mother.

To try to explain all that to Michael, she'd have to ask him to leave his comfortable place of thinking everything was fine and enter her world of nebulous worries. She wasn't sure she could do that to him again.

The one and only time Michael had been really upset with her, upset enough to shout and curse and throw things around, was the last time she talked about how painful her relationship with her mother had been.

"Get over it already," he'd said. "I'm sorry, but problems are real things. Abuse. Drinking. Neglect. Poverty." He'd paused, as if wondering if he should say more, then blew out a breath. "I'm sorry, Jenny. The fact that your mother didn't talk to you just isn't that significant."

Before he could see the pain his words inflicted on her, or the tears she couldn't control, she turned away.

Later, she realized he wasn't being insensitive. Well, maybe a little bit. But he truly was a good man, and she couldn't blame him for not *getting* her childhood scars. Someone who came from a large boisterous family that lived and loved with enthusiasm, couldn't comprehend the stark loneliness and sense of isolation that had dogged her childhood.

Maybe it would've been different if Daddy hadn't died, Jenny thought. Maybe if mother hadn't been saddled with two girls to raise all by herself, she could've been more like Mrs. Corbett.

Jenny shook herself as a cool breeze blew across the porch and goosebumps erupted on her bare arms. She could spend an eternity playing the what-if game. And another eternity trying to get the courage to talk to Michael about this again.

She glanced at his profile, a dark silhouette against the pale glow of the street light on the corner. Knowing him, he was probably mentally wrestling with some problem at work. He'd stop and listen if she asked. Did she dare?

"You know, it's funny." Jenny pushed her barefoot against the cool concrete of the porch, making the swing slowly sway back and forth. "I've been thinking lately..."

"Oh no," Michael said with a slight grin. "Look out world, Jenny is thinking again."

"Be serious." Jenny frowned at him and then glanced away. Maybe it would be easier if she didn't look at him. "What I've been thinking about is how much life is the same even though circumstances are different."

"I don't follow."

"You know. What happens to people in their lifetime may be different, but people are still people. Their reactions to life experiences are often the same." Jenny glanced at Michael, but a frown furrowed his brow. She sighed. "I mean. Well, take for example me and my mother. Sometimes, right in the middle of the kids and the hassles and the responsibility, I can sense what she must have felt as a young mother raising kids. And while it's the same on some levels it's still different."

"Yeah. We have more kids."

She smacked him. "Be serious."

"Okay." He ran a hand across the back of her neck. "I didn't know all that childhood mess was still bothering you."

"I try not to think about it." She shrugged. "But sometimes I can't help it."

"Does thinking help? Does it change anything?" His tone wasn't accusing, but Jenny had to tamp down a surge of resentment.

"It might help me to understand. To salvage something before it's too late."

Before she could say any more, the front door banged open.

"Phone, Mom," six-year-old Danny announced in a voice reserved for what he called his "I'm a big boy" situations.

"Okay." Jenny got up, gave Michael a pat on the shoulder, then followed her son into the house.

After shooing Danny back to bed, she picked up the phone receiver, anticipating what she was going to say to the person who chose such an inopportune time to sell her magazines. "Hello."

"Oh Jenny! I'm so glad you're home." The voice

crackled along with the static on the line that carried it over hundreds of miles, but Jenny still recognized her sister. Her heart began to pound in heavy thumps as she caught the unmistakable note of rising hysteria. "Cheryl. What is it?"

"It's Ma. She's had a heart attack."

"Oh my God! What? How is she?"

"She's alive. We got her to the hospital in time. The doctor's with her now." Cheryl's voice became strangled with emotion. "Oh Jenny. I'm so scared. Can you come home? I need you."

The words stunned Jenny into a momentary silence. She wasn't sure if it was the news or the urgency she heard in her older sister's voice. It was the first time Jenny could ever remember her sister saying she needed her. It had always been the other way around. "Whoa, Cheryl. Slow down. Of course, I'll come. But I might not be able to get there until tomorrow. Will you be all right until then?"

"Yes. Call Greg and let him know your flight information. One of us will meet you."

"Okay. I'm not sure I want to hang up, but I don't know what to say."

"Don't say anything. Just come."

Abruptly, the line went dead, and Jenny slowly cradled the receiver. *Oh, Michael what am I going to do?*

She turned and he was there.

"It's Mother," Jenny said, her voice muffled in his chest; her tears dampening his shirt.

"I guessed as much." Michael ran a soothing hand through her hair.

They stood that way for a long moment, then she pulled away. "I'm sorry. I didn't think I'd just fall apart like this."

"It's okay." Michael gently traced a line down her cheek where a tear had just traveled. "Go to New York. I'll take care of things here."

Early the following afternoon, Jenny was on a plane headed north. Settling back against the seat, she closed her eyes, hoping for a nap. She hadn't slept the night before and exhaustion washed over her in huge waves. If only she could stop worrying. Stop thinking.

Her thoughts of her mother had taken her into strange unexplored areas recently. One minute she'd see her mother as a closed off shell of a person who had nothing to offer a frightened, confused child who was missing her Daddy and wondering where he had gone. Jenny the child would walk into the kitchen of her past. "Mommy?"

"Not now, Jenny. Can't you see I'm busy. I worked all day. I'm exhausted, and I still have to fix dinner. Go help your sister set the table."

Then, in the midst of her Deja vu, Jenny would

become the mother, and she'd be pushing her own kids away. She'd be crying and telling them to go away before they took everything out of her.

Realizing she wasn't going to be able to sleep, Jenny snatched the magazine out of the pocket in the seat in front of her and started leafing through it. Anything, even ads for beauty products she would never use, would be better than allowing her mind to continue on that tortuous path.

When Jenny's plane landed at LaGuardia, Cheryl was at the gate to meet her, and the two sisters embraced awkwardly. It had been a long time. Almost five years.

"How was the flight?" Cheryl asked as they threaded their way through the crowds bustling around the busy airport.

"It was okay." Jenny wished that they were the kind of sisters who could share idle chatter about the trip. Perhaps have a good chuckle over the guy who'd made a pass at her on the plane. But that type of conversation didn't come naturally for them. They'd never shared much. At times her sister, who was three years older, had seemed as remote and unapproachable as their mother.

"How's Mama?" Jenny asked.

"Holding her own for now. The doctor said the next few days will make the difference."

Jenny nodded and dug in her purse for her baggage checks. "Okay. Let's get my luggage and go on to the hospital."

Cheryl took charge with an older sister efficiency that Jenny remembered well, and soon they were settled in Cheryl's old station wagon, with her suitcase in the back and a discarded McDonald's drink cup on the floor of the passenger side. "Sorry about the mess," Cheryl said, grabbing the offending cup and tossing it over her shoulder to the backseat. "With all that's been going on ... "

"It's okay," Jenny said. "It's not like I haven't seen the same in my car."

Cheryl gave her a wan smile and pulled away from the curb.

As the car joined the stream of traffic on Grand Central parkway and rumbled along, a silence fell between the sisters, but it wasn't a comfortable silence. Jenny watched billboards and buildings flash by, and tried to think of something, anything, to say. It hadn't always been like this. These long painful silences. There'd been a time, a long time ago, when they'd talked. When they'd laughed together over crazy little things. All of them. Even her mother. But that had been before ...

Even though Jenny had only been five when her father died, she could still remember what their life had been like before that fateful day. And she could still remember the abrupt change that occurred almost the very moment they received the news. All the gaiety and laughter had vanished. It didn't fade away like the end of a record slowly ebbing into silence. It merely stopped short, leaving that vast silence and emptiness in the house and deep inside her soul.

The ensuing years had merged into an endless chain of days linked together with work, worry, and more work on the part of her mother, and Jenny was left adrift and reeling. So much about that new way of living had been so unreal to her childish mind.

Through those growing-up years, all she'd ever wanted was to be able to talk to her mother about the confusion. The loneliness. The sadness. But there never seemed to be any time to talk.

Today, despite how hard Jenny tried to deny it, there was still a frightened little girl inside her who longed for the comfort of her mother's arms as she cried herself to sleep.

"Here we are." Cheryl's voice pulled her out of her reverie, and Jenny looked through the windshield to see the sign for Mt. Sanai hospital.

"Oh my," Jenny said. "That was quick."

"Not all that quick." Cheryl gave her a wry smile. "You were lost in thought for the past half hour."

"Sorry."

"No worries." Cheryl pulled into the parking lot, found an open spot, and turned off the engine. "Ready?"

Jenny smiled ruefully. "Is anyone ever truly ready?"

Cheryl shrugged. "I'm afraid that's a little heavy for me right now."

"That's all right. It was strictly rhetorical."

Walking into the ICU cubicle where her mother was lying on a raised hospital bed, Jenny's initial shock quickly gave way to an overwhelming surge of fear and apprehension. Her mother looked so small. So frail. And all those tubes and wires in her arms, her nose, attached to her chest. It was almost obscene. Jenny's eyes filled with tears as she searched the ashen face for signs of life. "Are you sure she's okay?" she asked Cheryl in a soft whisper.

"Yes. She's heavily sedated. So, she'll be sleeping most of the time. But her heartbeat is now closer to normal. The doctor said she's stronger than most of his patients."

Yes. She's always been strong, Jenny thought. Didn't everyone say so? "That Mrs. Tucker. She's so brave. She's so strong. And she's done such a fine job of raising those two girls all by herself."

The abrupt stab of bitterness that accompanied that thought made Jenny wonder if she was in the middle of some sort of emotional ping pong game, playing both sides of the table. It was as if her whole life, past and present, had been stirred together, and she wasn't sure what emotion was going to surface next.

Still, she had no right to sit in judgment of her mother's life.

Did she?

"Come on." Cheryl put her hand on Jenny's shoulder, urging her toward the door. "Let's go to the lounge. The nurse will call us if there's any change."

————

The passage of time became a blur in Jenny's mind. How many days had it been already? Three? Four? And she couldn't remember what she'd said to her sister or brother-in-law when they sat together in the waiting area. Or what they had done when they weren't sitting vigil at the bedside. Or when she had last slept. Her days and nights were filled with torments of that terrible fear that her mother might die. Then it would be too late for them both. Too late for any kind of reconciliation. The waiting was taking an immeasurable toll on Cheryl as well. Jenny could see it in the grim set of her sister's jaw and the taut lines of worry around her eyes.

Wishing she could do something, Jenny

watched her sister leaf through a magazine then plop it down on the table in front of the sofa where she was sitting. Maybe they could talk. She got up from the chair and went over to the small sofa. "Cheryl, I—"

"Don't touch me!" The vehemence in Cheryl's voice hit Jenny with a force of a battering ram. "I ... I don't understand. What's wrong?"

"Part of the reason she's here is because of you."

"Wait a minute!"

"No. It's time you heard this. You don't know how much it upset her when you moved away. It was like you were cutting us out of your life. She's never been the same since." Cheryl paused. "I was a fool to think things would be different now."

Jenny's mind whirled in confusion, and she grabbed the first clear thought that came to her. "Doesn't the accused at least get a chance to defend herself."

Cheryl glared. "You aren't on trial."

"Then why does it feel like I am?"

Cheryl took a long moment before responding, and Jenny felt the anger build. How dare she?

"Maybe I shouldn't have—"

"You're damn right you shouldn't have." Jenny fought to keep her voice below shouting level. "Did you ever consider that she had a part in it too? She's the one who pushed me away all those years. She wouldn't talk about Daddy. Or how we were all feeling. She kept her emotions locked up inside and us locked out."

"Jenny, that was a long time ago. It doesn't matter."

"But it does! Don't you see? That's why I moved away. That's why I still hurt so bad inside every time I think about our childhood."

Even Jenny was surprised at the bitterness in her voice, and the two sisters simply looked at each other as the words hung between them, like the last notes of a song ending and slipping into silence.

Finally, Cheryl reached out to touch Jenny's hand, but Jenny pulled away and averted her eyes.

After another long moment, Cheryl spoke softly. "I'm sorry. I shouldn't have lashed out at you."

Jenny shrugged.

"Please, can we just talk?"

"What's there to say? It's obvious you don't feel the same way I do about all this mess."

"My God, Jenny! We grew up together. Remember? We went through the same things. Don't you think it affected me to? But there came a time when I put everything away."

"It's not as simple as packing away last year's clothes."

"I know. I didn't say it was easy. I just said I did it."

The gentleness in Cheryl's voice broke Jenny's last wall of defense. Tears started to slip unheeded out of her eyes and roll in a warm stream down her face. "How?" she asked. "How did you get past it?"

Cheryl tentatively reached out a hand and this time Jenny didn't pull away. "I can't tell you how to put your monsters to rest," Cheryl said. "That's something you have to do by yourself. Or long term, with a therapist."

Jenny looked up in surprise. "Did you? See a therapist?"

Cheryl nodded. "For about a year. Right after you left."

"Why didn't you ever tell me?"

"We haven't exactly talked a lot. Remember?"

That brought a small smile. "But what if ... what if ... " Jenny waved a hand in a vague gesture in the direction of their mother's room. "What if we don't have any more time?"

Cheryl held her gaze for a long moment, then said, "Maybe you can start today with forgiving her."

"Is that all there is to it? Just forgive her and all the pain will go away?"

Cheryl shrugged. "Maybe you have to forgive yourself too."

"What?" Again, her volume threatened to be too loud for a hospital waiting room.

"Don't get mad. Just think for a minute. You've harbored judgments about mother for years. Maybe part of the healing is letting go of all that. Then forgiving yourself for hanging on to the negativity for so long. Seems like it's been your favorite chew toy for as long as I can remember."

Jenny opened her mouth to blurt an angry response, but then clamped her lips tight. Maybe Cheryl had a point. Not a point that fell pleasantly on Jenny's ears, but just maybe a good one. She swallowed hard, then stood. "I'm going to go check on Mama."

"Okay. I'm ready to go home. I'll see you in the morning."

Jenny nodded, then turned to walk down the dim corridor, the low murmur of voices at the nurses' station barely a distraction as she passed. She entered the darkness of her mother's room that was lit only by the blue screen of the monitor. In the background, she heard the steady tick, tick, tick of the monitor and the faint whisper of breath moving in and out of her mother's body. She walked to the bed and stood there, studying the intricate pattern of lines the years had etched on her mother's face. In repose, it was the face of a stranger, and Jenny felt the need to memorize every wrinkle, is if

49

they made some significant statement about all that stood between them. Maybe they did, and maybe she could smooth it all away with a touch of her hand.

A sudden erratic change in her mother's breathing triggered an alarm and she pulled her hand back. *Dear god! Not now!*

Abruptly, the door opened to admit a nurse who flicked on the overhead lights and hurried over to the bed, bringing a chill into the room with her crisp, no-nonsense efficiency.

"Is she okay?" Jenny asked.

Intent on checking the wires, tubes, and the monitor, the nurse seemed oblivious to Jenny's presence, and Jenny shifted from foot to foot, waiting for an answer. The fear was like some great beast gnawing away at her stomach.

Finally, when Jenny thought she wouldn't be able to stand it any longer, the nurse finished checking the intricate equipment.

"Everything's okay," the nurse said, barely glancing at Jenny as she passed. "Must have been an anomaly. Her vitals are fine now."

"Oh." The word died on Jenny's lips as the nurse left and closed the door.

Through a mist of fear and anguish, Jenny recognized a tinge of anger too. She stalked over and turned the lights off, hoping the darkness would bring back a bit of the peace she'd felt before the alarm had sounded. She was angry with the nurse who seemed not to care that this was a person in the bed. A woman. A mother, who deserved more than cool efficiency and a sterile environment in which to die.

That last word hammered away in Jenny's mind.

It was true. Her mother could die. And the worst indignity of all was that it could happen while her mother still thought Jenny was as unfeeling as the nurse. Hot tears welled in Jenny's eyes, and she felt a great wrenching in her chest, like a great beast was tearing out her heart.

Reaching over, she picked up her mother's hand and lightly touched the wrinkled parchment-like skin with soft fingertips. Then the tears broke loose and ran freely down her cheeks, splashing on the entwined hands, one young and one old.

"Oh Mama!" The cry hung in the room like filmy layers of smoke. "You can't die Mama. Not now. I ... I need you. I ... I love you. Please! Please forgive me."

For a moment, Jenny held her breath wondering if her mother had even heard the words. Then she thought she felt the hint of pressure against her fingers. Was that a sign from her mother or merely an involuntary reflex?

It did her heart good to believe that it had been a sign. And if her mother lived—No. When her mother came through this with more life to live, Jenny would say the words again.

WHERE'S DADDY?

I TOOK my son's hand and walked slowly to the front of the viewing room of the funeral parlor. He didn't understand what we were there for. At least, I didn't think he did. How much can a five-year-old comprehend? He knew I was upset, as were most of the people here, tears freely flowing down cheeks of all ages and emotions of high intensity sparking the atmosphere like downed power lines.

Kids pick up on emotions that crowd a room.

We stopped at the table filled with pictures of Jim that were nestled amid vases of flowers; a colorful array of yellow carnations, pink sweet peas, and bold, blue delphiniums. I'd made this arrangement myself, choosing the photographs and the flowers with great care. Jim smiled out of every picture frame, and the flowers appeared to be smiling too.

There was no casket for this simple memorial service that would start in a little while. There hadn't been enough of Jim left to put in a casket. Not long after those officers had come to my door to deliver the most devastating news of my life, a duffel bag with Jim's effects was delivered to me. I didn't open it. I didn't want to see what was inside. I didn't want his dog tags or any Army memento at this service, so I shoved it all away in a closet. Back behind the suits Jim would never wear again.

Anger rumbled through me as I remembered that horrible day.

Bobby tugged at my hand, momentarily tugging me away from the memory. "Why isn't daddy here?"

I gulped. "He can't be here. He's ... gone." I could hardly squeeze the words past the constriction in my throat. Each one threatened to choke me.

"Gone where?"

Oh God! How can I tell this child his father is in a million pieces somewhere in that godforsaken place the Army had sent him? I took a breath, then tried for a comforting smile. "Honey, I told you. Daddy died. He's in heaven."

"With Grandma?"

"Yes. With Grandma."

Bobby looked around again. "But, we saw Grandma. Before she went to heaven. In a box. Where's Daddy's box?"

At first, I didn't know what Bobby meant, but then I realized. He was remembering my mother's funeral. That had been a year ago, and I'd hoped Bobby had forgotten the details. But he hadn't.

Jim hadn't wanted me to take Bobby to the funeral parlor where my mother was laid out. "He's only four," Jim had said. "He doesn't need to see a dead body."

Jim didn't understand that need. When his grandfather had died, Jim was only three and his parents had deemed him too young to go to the funeral. But I knew from counseling children and teens that they needed funerals and memorial services. Whatever might give them concrete proof that their loved one had not just stopped visiting for some unknown reason. Death, without all the trappings of funerals, of mourning, was just too obscure.

I looked at my boy today. Now five. Who so desperately needed to see a dead body. Still, I couldn't tell him the horrible truth. Not today. Maybe later. Twenty years later. Or maybe not at all. Maybe he doesn't ever need that mental image that I can't shake no matter how hard I try.

Over a week ago, the base commander had come to my door to tell me about Jim. About the bomb that had taken his life, along with the two other men in the Humvee in Iraq. I asked when his body would be sent back to the States, and the man had just looked at me for the longest moment with the saddest expression. Then he glanced away before he said, "I'm sorry Mrs. Murphy. Your husband's body ... It was ... There's nothing left."

"Nothing? How can there be nothing?"

He looked at me again. "Trust me. You don't want to know the details."

"Yes, I do! Yes, I do!" I screamed the words over and over until he finally told me, and I visualized this great explosion of blood and bone and flesh. A human being turned into a macabre form of confetti, carried by the wind to be scattered over rocks and dust.

That's when I threw up on the officer's shoes.

Now, I felt like throwing up again, and I swallowed the bile that burned in my throat.

Helen stepped over and touched my arm. "Can I take Bobby for a little while?"

I gave my mother-in-law a thankful smile and passed the soft, pink hand over to her work-roughened one. "Grandma would like to spend some time with you," I said to Bobby. "Is that okay with you?"

Bobby nodded, then looked up at Helen. "Can we get cookies? I saw some." He gestured with his free hand to doorway in a far back corner of the room. The doorway led to another small room where refreshments were set up, courtesy of the funeral parlor and a few of my friends who thought chocolate would be needed.

Lots of chocolate.

And wine.

Lots of wine.

I watched Helen lead Bobby away, then glanced around the room, noticing Frank sitting alone. For a moment, I considered going to sit by him, but something in the rigid way he held his body cautioned me off. My father-in-law came from a long line of good country people, living on the farm where Frank's grandfather had first tilled the land and raised corn. Jim had hoped to eventually move back to the farm where he'd grown into a man. He wanted to raise his own son there, but that hope had been shattered as quickly as his body.

It was obvious that Frank was equally shattered, but he would not want to break into emotional pieces in front of anyone else, not even me, whom he had welcomed into the family with open arms at our first meeting.

Ten days had passed since we had gotten the news, and Jim's parents had flown from Indiana to Killeen, Texas where we lived in military housing. In those ten days, Frank had verbalized little, but his eyes were not silent. The pain reflected in those deep blue eyes, so much like Jim's, had stabbed me so deeply that at times I'd wanted to run. Other times I just wanted to go and hold this dear man. Helen, who knew me so well and recognized my impulse, would give a slight shake of her head when our eyes met, so I would simply give Frank a slight smile and he would nod in return.

As I looked at the tall, strong man today, I hoped that he was able to let his emotions tumble out when he and Helen were alone. Otherwise, if they were contained inside forever, they would fester and sour, eventually rotting his heart and his soul.

I turned and made my way toward the back of the room, stopping frequently to acknowledge hugs and offerings of condolence. Afraid of what emotions might escape my rigid control, I kept those contacts brief, sometimes not even registering to whom I was speaking.

My friend Sharla sat alone in the last pew, and she offered a tentative smile as I drew near. I slid in beside her, and she reached out to take my hand in a strong grip. "You holding up?" she asked.

"By my fingertips."

She squeezed my hand a little harder for a moment, then eased the pressure. "You'll make it. You're strong."

I didn't openly deny her words, but inside I was

screaming. I hadn't felt strong since Jim had left for his latest tour in Iraq. I pretended for his sake. Seeing him off with a smile and affirmation that we would be fine while he was gone. But the truth was that every time he left, I would become that insecure, apprehensive person I'd been before I'd met him. The only saving grace was that he would always return, and all would be okay again. But this time he was not coming home.

Nothing was going to be okay again.

A tear slipped out of my eye, then another, and another, until they made a warm river down my cheeks. Afraid that this crack in the dam would lead to a total collapse of the wall between me and a flood of emotion that would drown me, I pulled away from the comfort of my friend. "Need to check on Bobby."

"Sure," Sharla said. "I'll catch up to you later."

As I slid out of the pew, I mentally thanked God for this friendship. Sharla was another military wife, so she knew, really knew, what the life was about.

How we were always perched on a precipice.

How tragedy could strike at any time.

In the days since my tragedy had struck, she'd come over several times with meals. Chicken and dumplings and macaroni and cheese; comfort foods that Sharla knew I loved. Even though Bobby was still grappling with the tension in the house and trying to understand that his father had died, he had little difficulty eating the offerings. I'd hardly been able to force a bite down a throat that was raw from all the tears I'd swallowed.

The funeral director had arranged for a chaplain from a nearby hospital to come to conduct the memorial service. I'd declined the offer of the base chaplain. I didn't want a military service. I didn't want to hear what a hero Jim had been. Dying on a battlefield was not my idea of heroism, and I wanted the Army to have no part in this day. This day was for Jim the husband. Jim the father. Not Jim the soldier.

Chaplain Dave was a gray-haired man with a comforting presence, and he did not even blanch when I told him that we were not church goers. I didn't tell him that I was not sure about God at this point—that would have made the man blanch. I wasn't exactly mad at God. I didn't blame Him for what had happened to Jim. I was just spiritually numb, and I didn't know where God was for me.

The chaplain talked to me, and to Jim's parents, to get a sense of who Jim had been and pulled it all together for a nice service. At least that's what my friends told me later. I was there, yet I wasn't. I couldn't seem to hold on to words or sentences that were said in honor of Jim's memory. They seemed to float away like wisps of smoke coming out of the Chaplain's mouth.

Shortly after the words of the last prayer fell into a painful silence, people started slipping away, finally leaving just me and Sharla here. Frank and Helen had taken Bobby back to the house.

"You sure you want to do this?" Sharla gestured to the array of pictures and flowers I was going to take apart. "I could. Or the funeral director ... "

She let the rest of the sentence fade, and I gave her a weak smile. "I know. I already told him to donate the flowers to people at the hospital. The one where the chaplain works. He said women on the oncology ward would like them."

Sharla nodded. "I could still help with the pictures."

I shook my head. "Go home. Hug your husband and be thankful that you have him."

Sharla nodded again, tears brimming in her eyes. "I'm so very sorry."

"I know." The words were soft, choked, and Sharla wrapped me in strong arms. We stood there for long moments, just holding each other. Then she stepped back. Gave my shoulders a squeeze. Turned, and left.

I sat in the front pew of the small chapel and looked at all the pictures of Jim. Even though I'd wanted nothing tied to the military at this service,

Jim had spent too many years in the Army not to have one or two photos of him in uniform, but I glanced past them quickly, focusing slowly and deliberately on the others. Both of us acting silly at our graduation party. Him sitting on the steps of our high school. Had he been saying goodbye? I couldn't remember. He'd enlisted shortly after that, and we'd been separated for too many of the ensuing months.

I'd been angry, but I never told him. He was so proud of serving his country; I couldn't slap him with my anger. And really, there was no danger, was there?

Then came Iraq.

Wiping away the tears that were trailing down my cheeks, I shook those thoughts aside and looked at our wedding photo. I'd chosen the one of us laughing and pushing cake in each other's mouths. Through the years, we'd done a lot of laughing as we celebrated milestones and events. Ten years of laughing at anything and everything.

Then came Iraq.

The last picture was of Jim holding Bobby the first day we had the baby home with us. Jim was so thrilled to have a baby, a son, that I wondered if I'd ever get to hold our child again. Even though he couldn't feed the baby, Jim did everything else. He wasn't afraid of bathing him, and he wasn't reluctant to change diapers. If Jim could have lactated, he probably would have taken over feeding too. We had five glorious years of sharing parenthood whenever Jim was home from deployment.

Then came Iraq.

You can't keep looping back to that, I told myself. No matter how frustrated or angry you are, it won't change a thing.

I brushed more tears away and sighed deeply. It was time.

At the house, I put the pictures on the credenza in the living room. Then I went into my bedroom. There, I took all the mementoes Jim had gathered from his trips to other countries during his service from the top of his bureau and put them in a box. That box went into my closet. Shoved way back on the top shelf where I'd put the things the officer had given me.

Someday I'd take the boxes out. Open them and show everything to Bobby. I'd tell Bobby what had really happened to his father. But not today. Not any day real soon. Let him be a child a little while longer, untouched by a realization that his father had died in vain.

That was the worst part.

CROSSING THE THRESHOLD

FIRST PUBLISHED IN THE CORNER CAFÉ ANTHOLOGY

FRANK PUSHED OPEN THE DOOR, expecting to walk into his favorite tavern. He stopped just inside the doorway and looked around for the bar. For the bartender. For the stevedores who always claimed the far end of the bar and dared anyone to try to take one of their seats. He was looking for a guy, a dame, and a drink, not necessarily in that order. A much too chipper young thing flitted toward him like some kind of bird. In fact, she could have been a canary with that bold yellow shirt. She was wearing short pants with her gams hanging out for everyone to see. Not that they were bad looking gams, long and lean, but why show some leg if you aren't going to show some tits?

"Welcome to the Corner Café," the bright little

thing said. "What can I get you? Mocha? A latte? Espresso?"

Frank removed his fedora—a gentleman always does that when in the presence of a lady, even one as annoying as this. "Don't know what you're saying there, girlie. Where's Mickey?"

"Mouse?"

Frank shook his head, hoping maybe the action would rewind whatever filmstrip was playing behind his eyeballs. "Look lady, stop stalling around. What happened to the Watering Hole? And where's Mickey, the owner?"

"I'm sorry, sir. Never heard of that place. Perhaps you're at the wrong location?"

"Listen. I been coming here every night for years. I could find it in my sleep."

"Maybe that's your problem," a man at a nearby table said. "Maybe you should wake up."

Frank touched the butt of the gun in the holster under his coat and shot the man a glare of steel. "Don't get wise with me. Do you know who you're talking to?"

"Yeah, some joker who just came from a costume party. Who you supposed to be? Sam Spade?"

Frank shifted to take a step toward the man. He'd teach him to make fun of Frank Perelli. The girl put a restraining hand on his arm. "Please, sir, we don't want any trouble."

Frank stopped, took a breath to curb his urge to deck the guy, and cast another careful look around at the people seated at tables that were scattered around the room. Not a trench coat or zoot suit in sight. These people were wearing the oddest clothing. Some men had short pants that looked like knickers, but what grown man would ever wear knickers? And so many of them were sporting what looked like underwear shirts. Frank looked closer at the man who had heckled him. His underwear shirt was red and had some writing on it. Metallica?

What the hell was a Metallica? Frank looked back at the girl. "Who are all these funny-looking people?"

"These?" The girl followed his sweeping gesture. "Well, these are some of our regulars. They come in for coffee every day."

Coffee? Frank glanced at where the bar used to be with the big mirror below the nude painting. There was some kind of menu posted, everything written in some flowery script his maiden aunt used to write her letters. He took another sweep of the room. *Crazy.* "Why are these people dressed like that? I haven't seen this much skin since I busted that porno outfit."

"Are you a cop?" The girl asked.

"No. Gumshoe."

She gave him a funny look. "Pardon me? You have gum on your shoe?"

Frank raised one of his feet to check the sole of his wingtip. Nothing there. She continued to look at him with a frown wrinkling her brow. He continued to look at her, wondering what the hell was happening here. She was a cute little thing, sparkling blue eyes, hair that shimmered gold in the light; that frown the only thing marring flawless skin. No sign of any weird antennae. "You from some other planet you don't know from gumshoe?"

"No sir. I'm from right here in Chicago. Born and raised. And I have no idea what you're talking about."

Frank pulled out his wallet and showed her his license. "I'm a P.I."

"Oh, a private investigator." A smile replaced her frown. "Are you on a case? Can I help? I've always wanted to be a PI. Sounds so ... you know ... dramatic ... exciting ... adventurous."

"It's work, girlie. Plain and simple. Lots of pounding the pavement trying to track down some wiseguy or another."

"Are you tracking someone now?"

"Yeah. Paul Ricca. They call him The Waiter. Heard he was meeting up with Johnny Roselli to do some business. Bringing their Hollywood extortion business to Chicago. Can't have that."

"Our waiter is Todd, and I've never heard of a Johnny Roselli." The girl cocked one hip. "This is a nice quiet coffee shop. So, you better just take your nonsense and get out of here."

Frank took one more look around, then shrugged. What the hell. He wasn't getting anywhere in this joint. Maybe if he went out and came back in, he'd be where he belonged. He tipped his hat to the girl and turned to head to the door.

The girl motioned to a man at a back table. He took out a cell phone and placed a call.

Outside, Frank paused to shake out a Lucky and strike a match. He'd barely touched the flame to the end of the cigarette, when he felt a sudden movement behind him. He whirled, but not in time to see what hit him. He fell to the sidewalk, the cigarette slipping from between his lips and rolling across the pavement leaving a trail of sparks. He couldn't tell if the blackness was the night sky devoid of stars or unconsciousness sweeping toward him.

His last thought was, those damn Hollywood guys. What length they won't go to in order to get a guy.

BEYOND THE CRACK IN THE SIDEWALK

BEYOND THE CRACKED sidewalk and the telephone pole with layers of flyers in a rainbow of colors, and the patch of dry brown grass, there stood a ten-foot-high concrete-block wall, caked with dozens of coats of paint, reds bleeding through blues with streaks of yellow adding highlights like shafts of sunlight. A small shrine stood at the foot of the wall; burnt out candles lying on their sides amidst clusters of wilted brown flowers and a few tattered teddy bears. One word of graffiti filled the wall, red letters on a gold background: Rejoice!

Using the tips of her fingers, Hannah traced the letters. Rejoice? What was there to rejoice about? We should be happy that Carlos is gone? Happy that he's in heaven? That's what the priest had said at the funeral. Hannah had been shocked. No way would she ever be happy that Carlos was in heaven. It was only her love for Carlos that had kept her from running out of St. Vincent's Church the day they supposedly put his body and soul to rest. Was anyone's soul ever at rest? At peace?

Some people might think you couldn't fall in love in just a day, but Hannah believed it could happen. She'd known that Carlos existed for longer, but she'd only loved him for one day. He'd first approached her a little over a year ago, when she was trying to get food from a dumpster behind the Mexican restaurant on Main Street. She was short. He was tall, and he easily reached in to get the latest trash bag that might contain a few chips that weren't rubbery with spilled salsa. Chips that still crunched were always better than cold, soggy, leftover enchiladas.

"Here." He'd given her a grease-stained paper bag. "You look like you need these."

Without responding, she'd snatched the bag and dashed away. Her friend Angie had warned Hannah about men who liked to take advantage of homeless girls. The men who'd be so friendly, so charming and nice in order to prime them for sex and sex trafficking. So, even though this person — this boy who could hardly be called a man — didn't look dangerous, Hannah wasn't taking any chances. A few days after that, the boy had disappeared. She'd never even learned his name. After several months passed without her seeing him at St. Vincent's shelter or anyplace on the streets where the homeless kids gathered in hopes of scoring some handouts; she thought he'd moved on to another city.

Then one day he was back.

She was sitting on the rocky slope that led to a small creek. It was bridged by the overpass of the highway leading out of Pine Tree, Missouri, and she was staying a fair distance away from a cluster of other kids. She didn't know them, and it was better to ignore them, especially when the effects of booze or dope made them a real danger to someone alone. She heard some of them call out, and she turned to see the boy approaching the others. "Hey, Carlos," one rangy teen called out. "Wassup?"

Hannah watched him exchange a few high fives and thought the Spanish-sounding name suited the boy.

Carlos, who was still not yet a man, was tall and muscular and had eyes the color of ebony with hair to match. In a whole year she'd never forgotten those deep, dark eyes. Eventually, he made his way toward her. She saw a glint of white as he offered a smile. "Can I have a piece of this dirt?"

Not entirely ready to trust this boy with perfect white teeth and smooth cheeks a rich shade of burnt sienna, she nodded but didn't say anything. She pulled her stained denim jacket tight around her, partially as protection from the autumn chill and partially to create a barrier between herself and someone who scared and intrigued her in equal measures. Most of the kids she'd met since coming here from St. Louis two years ago didn't have good teeth. In fact, they'd probably not been to the dentist ever in their short, miserable lives. So how did a guy who had such a perfect smile end up here? He hunkered down beside her and pulled a grease-stained brown sack out of a pocket in his torn bomber jacket. "I found more chips." He held out the bag.

He'd remembered. After all this time, he'd remembered, but this time she didn't take the offering. Today, she wasn't starving. Only hungry. Hungry could decline food from a stranger.

Carlos didn't seem to mind. He also didn't go away. Settling into a more comfortable position, he opened the bag and started to munch on the chips. "I'm Carlos. I guess you heard." He gestured vaguely to the boys who had called him by name. "I remember you from before. A year ago, maybe? I had to leave. Just came back."

Short, simple comments that piqued Hannah's

curiosity. Where had he gone, and why did he come back? As if they were having a real conversation and she'd responded out loud, Carlos supplied the information. "My family is ... well, difficult. But I thought I could handle them. My Mom, uh, screaming at me all the time. Dad just ignoring her and me. So, I went back for a while. But it was even worse. Hated walking away again, but I just couldn't stand it. They say stress isn't good for you, right?"

He offered a smile, but she didn't smile back. A flare of anger surprised her. She shouldn't judge. Everybody's story was different, but really? Running away because his mother yelled and his father ignored him?

God, he should've been thrilled to be ignored.

Hannah would've been thrilled to be ignored.

Carlos held out the bag again, and she reached in to grab several chips. "What's your story?" he asked.

She looked at him, considering, then shook her head.

"Don't want to talk, eh? I'm good with that."

They sat for a while, laughter from the group of kids a short distance away getting loud and raucous at times, then softer, like the tide ebbing and flowing. Hannah's wave of anger also ebbed, and the tension of silence between her and Carlos eased.

She glanced up at his face for a moment, then quickly averted her eyes. Should she talk to this guy? Part of her wanted to. To let him see what was actually horrible enough to drive someone to the streets. Still, she hesitated. Did he really want to know what had brought her to this little town in the middle of nowhere?

Maybe he did, but she wasn't sure she was willing to tell him.

The last person she'd opened up to, her school counselor, hadn't believed her about what her step-father had been doing. It had taken months of ago-nizing for her to build up the courage to go to the counselor, and he'd turned on her. Called her par-ents. Of course, Allen, with his smiles and charm and feigned innocence, had lied about touching her —raping her.

God, even in her mind, Hannah hated to say those words. She hated to think about Allen. Or the scene at home later when her mother rained down a barrage of words so hurtful, they'd nailed Hannah to the floor for several minutes. Her mother actually believed that Hannah had led him on. What a hor-rible cliché. If Hannah hadn't been so stunned, she might have laughed.

"You're a clueless bitch." Hannah had thrown the words at her mother like darts before whirling and racing to her room, slamming and locking the door. She stayed in her bedroom for hours. Not leaving or opening her door, even when Allen pounded, shouting for her to come out. The wood creaked under his heavy fists, and she held her breath, hoping he wouldn't come crashing in.

The door held. So did the lock.

She stayed huddled on her bed until she was sure her mother and Allen were asleep. Then she shoved a couple shirts and some underwear in her backpack, adding her teddy bear at the last minute, grabbed money and a few personal things, and bolted.

The bus ticket to St. Louis cost twenty-five dollars. Twenty-five from the two-hundred Hannah had been saving for a new tablet, plus the fifty her friend Angie had given her.

The last call Hannah had made on her cell phone that night was to her friend, who hadn't hesitated to come in the middle of the night. Who hadn't hesitated about the money. Who understood when Hannah said they probably wouldn't be in contact again. Not for a long time. Hannah needed to be far away to be safe from Allen. That's when Angie had warned Hannah about the dangers on the streets and begged her to be careful. Be safe.

Leaving her friend had been one of the hardest things she'd had to do. Second only to smashing her phone so she couldn't be traced.

Hannah figured once she got to a place far away from Indiana, she'd get a job and start a new life. One that didn't include Allen or anyone like him.

Ending up homeless is this Podunk town out-side of the big city wasn't part of the plan she'd shared with her friend while they sat on the swings in that park so long ago. But, well, shit happens. And the money was long gone.

"Do you want to hang out together?" Carlos asked.

Hannah pulled away slightly, and he chuckled. "Not hitting on you. Just safety in numbers." He nodded toward the group of boys who had been passing a bottle of wine around and were now laughing louder in between what sounded like taunts. Tension sizzled in the air like electricity in a thunderstorm. "Pretty soon they're gonna start looking for their lamb."

Hannah didn't have to ask what he meant. She'd seen drunks turn on the weakest person too many times. Hell, Allen was a perfect example. She'd been his lamb for too long. After just a mo-ment's hesitation, she grabbed her backpack and took Carlos's hand. He gripped his small duffel with the other hand, and they scrabbled up the in-cline to the highway.

Away from the danger.

They walked to a park and found a bench

under some trees, far enough away from the park entrance that maybe they wouldn't be disturbed. They dropped their bags and sat down, both quiet for a while, Hannah finishing the chips. "You want to stay here?" Carlos asked. "It's not going to be too cold tonight." Hannah hesitated so long he added, "I won't touch you. I promise."

Wadding up the greasy bag from the chips, Hannah walked toward a green metal trashcan, using the time to consider a response. She did want to stay with him. And oddly enough, she wasn't so sure she didn't want him to touch her. How weird was that? A few kind words and two bags of tortilla chips and she was ready to be a kept woman. Or girl. Could she be a woman at sixteen? Well, maybe if she ...

Glad that her back was to him, she stifled a small smile. She had no idea what was causing her wild train of thought. The hint of winter in the air? Her abject loneliness? The possibility that there was more to Carlos than words?

Definitely not the weather.

She tossed the bag, wiped her hands on her frayed blue jeans, and went back to the bench. Carlos seemed unconcerned that she had taken so long to get rid of a single piece of trash, and he smiled at her as she took the space next to him. She sat there for a couple of minutes in silence, then scrounged in her backpack and pulled out her teddy bear. She hugged the tattered bear tight. "If you still want to hear my story, I'll tell you."

"Okay." The word was spoken softly with encouragement holding it up.

After a long moment, she started, letting the story spill out, a mere trickle at first in a faint voice that was not accustomed to saying so much all at one time. Then the words gained force as her emotions gained strength. While her river of pain ran on, she was only partially aware of his arm around her. Tentative at first, then strong and more firmly protective. He didn't say anything. Didn't ask any questions. Just held her, while she clutched her bear, until the words, and the tears, subsided.

Then he'd talked far into the night, wrapping her in words of caring and commitment. Words that made her feel safe for the first time in years. And words that told the horrible truth of his story. How wrong she'd been about his first revelation that had glossed over something so much worse.

Eventually, she fell asleep, feeling secure for the first time in years.

The sun had barely made a dent in the darkness, when Hannah felt something move under her head and she instantly woke up, taking a moment to remember where she was and who she was using for a pillow. Definitely not her teddy bear. She sat up abruptly.

"Hey. Didn't mean to disturb you." Carlos said. "Going to get us some breakfast."

"Want me to come with you?" Hannah asked. Not because she wondered if he meant breakfast for both of them. After last night, she knew. This boy/man was going to take care of her, and for the first time since she'd spent her last dime and still didn't have a job and ended up homeless, she had a glimmer of hope that things were going to be okay.

He shrugged into his bomber jacket that had ragged holes in the sleeves. "Nah. I'll bring back eggs and bacon and toast and hash browns."

She couldn't hide her eager anticipation, and he laughed. "Really. I wish I could. But I'll grab what I can find." He touched her cheek with his fingertips. "Wait for me here."

Hannah did. She waited almost two hours, hugging her dirty backpack to her belly and trying to tamp down the fear that had started as just a little irritation after the first half hour, but had grown to a raging inferno. Wasn't he coming back? Had she been duped? Again? Didn't he mean those things he'd said last night? This morning? Had it all been a lie?

Anger warred with worry, and then a siren screaming in the distance broke the battle of emotions. She listened as the reverberation drew nearer. It sounded like it was going down the street on the south side of the park.

The street that was bordered by the tall concrete wall where kids painted graffiti.

The street that held the restaurants where they could sometime snag some semi-fresh food from the dumpsters.

Jumping up, Hannah raced through the park, low-hanging branches from trees slapping her in the face as she blasted down the path. Reaching the street, she stopped cold at the sight of the red and blue pulsing lights of an ambulance and several cop cars askew on the road. She walked over to a couple of other kids she recognized from St. Vincent's. "What happened?"

"A man was shot," a girl said. "By the restaurant." She gestured down the street. "They don't know how he managed to get back here to the wall. It looks like he's dead."

Hannah moved to get a better view and saw a bomber jacket. The one with the sleeves ragged and torn.

On the ground.

On the body on the ground.

She started to bolt across the street, but strong arms grabbed her. "Don't," a deep baritone voice said, "if you don't want to get caught, walk away. It's just Carlos."

It's just Carlos? God! She whirled to see Joseph, an older boy who was often at the shelter. How could he say that? Pain stabbed Hannah so hard and so deep, she doubled over. She wanted to scream. To hit someone. To run. To do something, anything to take the pain away. But she knew she should do none of those things. Joseph was right. She couldn't risk drawing the attention of authorities, so she turned and stumbled her way back through the park, letting her tears run in a hot river down her cheeks.

Chest heaving from exertion and emotion, Hannah stopped at the bench where they'd spent the night; Carlos holding her against him, his warmth penetrating the thin layers of her clothing. Making her feel safe. Comforted. Almost happy. Where he had told her that he would be her friend. Forever if she wanted. And he would make sure that nobody ever hurt her again.

Now he was gone and so was her hope.

Hannah sat down to catch her breath. She opened her backpack to get a rag to wipe her ravaged face and saw her bear; the ragged brown teddy bear with one missing eye. It was the only thing she had left that connected her to a childhood that was good. The carefree time before her father died. Before Allen. She rubbed the soft fabric of the bear's ear and tried to straighten the yellow ribbon that had become a wrinkled, tangled mess from being shoved into the backpack, taken out, and shoved back in so many times. The bear had been her comfort during all the days and weeks and months of uncertainty and danger while living on the streets.

Then she'd had Carlos.

———

Three days later, a gleaming red SUV pulled up and parked beside the concrete wall. The woman in the driver's seat opened the door, but didn't get out. Although her face was in shadow, Hannah had a sense that the woman was sad. There was something about how she'd turned away from the sun and rested the weight of her hands on the steering wheel; something about her silent composure. From her vantage point across the street, Hannah watched the driver lean out the window and stretch her hand toward one of the burned-out candles.

After idling there for several minutes, the lady pulled slowly away. Hannah waited a few minutes, then walked over to the wall, crouching down and straightening her bear that had fallen sideways. She didn't know why she'd decided to put the bear here. The act hadn't brought relief from the horrible, wrenching grief that threatened to tear her apart, but she'd given in to the impulse.

Hannah went to the granite wall every day, cleaning out dead flowers and rearranging candles and other stuffed animals left there. She always half-expected to see the woman in the red car, but a whole week went by before she came again. This time, the lady got out of the vehicle, bringing flowers that she placed alongside the other mementos. This time, Hannah walked over to stand beside her. For several moments the woman didn't acknowledge Hannah's presence, but then she turned toward her. "Did you know my son? Carlos?"

Hannah met the woman's eyes and nodded.

"What's your name?"

Breaking eye contact, Hannah didn't answer. On the streets your name was protected as fiercely as your backpack. If people knew your name, they could sell it to the cops for the price of a pass on a minor drug bust. Then the cops would call parents. Maybe. But if they did, Hannah could end up back with her mother and Allen. Not that Hannah really thought this woman wished her any harm, but the years on the streets had taught her to be cautious.

Hannah had already guessed that the woman was his mother. The one Carlos had run away from, but she didn't fit the mental image Hannah had formed when he'd shared the real truth of his story.

About the drinking. About the abuse. About the inappropriate touching. Before hearing that, Hannah had never thought of a man, or a boy, being sexually abused, but it certainly provided a stronger motive for running away than just fleeing a mother who yelled too much. And she'd understood why he'd hidden his real motives so deep.

"How close were you? You and Carlos?" The question brought Hannah back to the moment, and she shrugged. Then the woman said. "I saw you at the funeral. When you came forward to pay your respects. By your demeaner, it appeared that you knew him more than just casually. Not something you could simply shrug away."

"What does it matter?" Hannah glared at the woman, her anger at knowing what she'd done to her son fueling the anger over the injustice of his death. "He's gone. Lost to us both. And what do you care anyway. It's not like you loved him. At least not the right way."

The slap was quick and painful, leaving Hannah's cheek stinging. They stared at each other for one brief moment, then the mother ran to her SUV, got in, and tore away from the curb, leaving a streak of black on the concrete and the pungent aroma of burnt rubber floating in her wake. Hannah gingerly touched her cheek, wondering if she deserved the physical reprimand. Then she started to laugh; a laugh that soon turned into gut-wrenching sobs.

She rocked and wept until a hand touched her shoulder. She flinched, shrugging away from the touch. It came again and she looked up. It was Joseph. "Come on," he said. "It's going to freeze tonight. Come to the shelter."

Knowing he was right, she followed him, hanging back just a bit to avoid having to talk. She didn't want to talk. Even when kids came to the little shrine, she didn't want to talk. Didn't want to share hugs. Offers of sympathy threatened to crack the façade she was trying so desperately to maintain. If it broke, if she broke, she wasn't sure she could put herself back together. She would be like Humpty Dumpty, smashed to bits.

Hannah had avoided St. Vincent's church shelter since the funeral. She didn't want to be in the same place with the priest who had said all those things about a person being happy in heaven, and who had kept insisting that everyone should rejoice that the person they loved was now there with God. Hannah didn't even know if Carlos believed all that crap. Heaven, and all that it represented, was a hard concept for people who were living the worst kind of hell here on earth.

She knew.

Hannah finished the stew that had been provided by shelter volunteers and carried the empty bowl back to the long metal counter where an older lady with blue hair flattened by a hair net was taking the dirty dishes. She, like most of the other volunteers, was nice enough, but the women smiled too much and asked too many questions, mostly about whether Hannah had enough soap or could they call her parents. Before this woman's smile could morph into a question, Hannah turned quickly away, only to stop short when she saw two uniformed police officers step through the door, a young woman and an older black man. He called out, "We need to talk to anyone who was at the scene of the shooting on Third Street last week."

Nobody responded, and Hannah felt a hand on her arm. She turned to see Joseph, who started to lead her back to the table, whispering in her ear to stay calm and don't look at the police. Hannah kept her gaze lowered and sat down next to Joseph. Then she felt a presence beside them and glanced over to see brightly polished boots and the bottom of blue pants. "You, young lady, did you see the shooting?" The question came from the male officer.

Hannah kept her gaze averted and shook her head. Then he asked how old she was. Before Hannah could respond, Joseph told the man that this was his younger sister. He could vouch for her.

In response to the question of why she was at that memorial site so much; was the deceased a relative, too? Joseph said, "Nope. Just a friend. And my sister here, well, she's a neat freak. Likes to tidy up all kinds of places."

In the silence that followed, Hannah dared to glance directly at the officer, hoping he was buying Joseph's story. Apparently, he did, but with a hint of reservation. The officer gave both of them a searching look, then advised them to find their parents and get off the streets. Hannah didn't respond, but Joseph smiled and nodded. "Yes, sir, officer. Thank you, officer."

Hannah nudged Joseph to get him to stop before he blew it. He'd managed to get her out of a potential jam, and she was grateful, but she didn't want the cop to reconsider his decision to walk away. When he didn't stop, she whispered a thank you to Joseph. Then she gave him a long, hard scrutiny, wondering if she should align herself with him for safety. But, no. He was older, harder than Carlos, and rumor had it he was into drugs. Even though Joseph could sweet-talk the police, Hannah needed to keep him at a distance. A good distance. She'd made a promise to Angie and to herself. No drugs. They would only lead her down a very dark hole. One much worse than the one where she was now.

———

When two weeks passed without any sign of the woman, Hannah thought maybe she wasn't coming back. After the last encounter, Hannah had dug the funeral program out of her backpack and read what she hadn't been able to read the day that he'd been buried: Carlos Ramirez, beloved son of Marie and Franco Ramirez. Still, Hannah resisted using the woman's name. It was easier to think of her as someone without a name. A person with a name was not able to commit the horrific acts Carlos had endured. At least, that's the way it worked in Hannah's mind.

On a gray, bleak day that threatened snow, Hannah shivered in the cold as she cleared empty drink cups, bits of paper, and other debris that had blown into the shrine. Then she heard the sound of tires on the pavement behind her. She looked over her shoulder to see the familiar figure emerge from the red vehicle. Continuing to straighten the candles and the bears, Hannah didn't look up when the woman stopped beside her, standing quietly in front of the make-shift memorial for several minutes. When the woman finally spoke, the words tumbled out of her mouth like little kids kept indoors too long running out of a house. "When Carlos left the last time, it was the push I needed. I went to rehab. Started counseling. I'm changing. I wanted to find him. To tell him. But the counselor suggested waiting until I was a little more stable."

She gave a strangled cry. "I waited too long."

"Well, boo-hoo." Hannah stood and whirled on the woman, who gave her a startled look and opened her mouth to speak. Whatever she was about to say, Hannah knew it would be something along the lines of, "How dare you?"

Well, she dared a lot right now. "You tell me this sad story, and I'm supposed to feel sorry for you? What about Carlos? What about his story?"

The color drained from the woman's face. "How much do you know?"

Hannah held her answer back. Let the woman suffer. Hannah was not going to satisfy the woman's curiosity, or her obvious need for some kind of shared grief. If indeed that was what she was pushing for. If not, why did she keep coming back? Back here where she didn't belong. This was the place for Hannah to gather with the other street kids who had known Carlos. Let the woman gather with her friends. If she had any.

Hannah strode away and purposely avoided the woman after that. When she was at the wall and saw the red car approaching, she left. She could come back later to clean up the memorial site. Hannah was always a bit surprised each time she saw the woman after that last time they'd spoken. She'd thought the woman would give up, but she didn't, and Hannah continued to wonder why. If the woman still hoped to make some kind of connection, well, she could forget that idea. There was no way Hannah was going to ease the woman's guilt by offering any compassion. Let her rot in hell.

Then one day the woman surprised her by arriving on foot. Hannah was gathering burned out candles and didn't see the woman until she was almost next to her. She dropped the candles and started to walk away. "Wait," the woman called out. "Please. Just hear me out."

Hannah slowed her steps, then stopped, but didn't turn around.

"Thank you for caring for my son. And, well, caring for this place."

Hannah didn't respond, but the words softened her anger just a bit, and tears welled in her eyes. Still, this was not going to be a Hallmark moment. She was not going to rush into this woman's arms, with everyone living happily ever after.

"Well, that's all I wanted to say."

Hannah heard footsteps fading behind her. The woman was leaving. Good. Maybe she wouldn't come back. Maybe she was done acting like she really cared. Hannah swiped at a tear that had dared to slip out of her eye, glad the woman was not there to see the sign of weakness.

Late autumn turned into winter and survival on the streets became harder and harder. Hannah had managed to snag a quilted vest from a recent donation to St. Vincent's, but that and her denim jacket hardly provided much protection from the cold that penetrated deep into her bones and left her fingers cracked and raw. Still, she went to the wall most days, and she never saw the woman again. Sometimes, when she let a small part of her heart soften, she wondered if the woman had ever found peace. If anyone in this miserable world ever found any peace.

The days and weeks passed in a blur of trying to find food and trying to keep the memorial for Carlos as neat as she could.

This day, Hannah stood at the wall, shivering in the cold, burying her hands in her armpits to keep them warm. All the flowers had died weeks ago, and nobody brought any more. Probably because there were none to be picked in the parks, and who could buy flowers when they couldn't buy food? She looked down at the crack in the sidewalk. It had grown deeper, wider, as though whatever was left of her friend could at last slip through and escape the pain, the hopelessness of those who came here. "Carlos," she whispered, "I don't know what to do. I can't survive another winter on the streets. Please. If there is any fragment of your spirit here, help me."

Then the snow started. Soft, lovely flakes that drifted slowly down, and Hannah lifted her face to let them blanket her cheeks and nose and forehead. She remembered doing that as a child. How much she enjoyed doing that. Playing outside with her mother and father, catching snowflakes on their tongues and building snow-people; men and women and little girls. Was it possible to recapture the peace and joy the family had shared then? Before he'd died, and her life had turned to hell?

What would it take?

A simple phone call? That's what that blue-haired lady at St. Vincent's always said. Just call your parents. They care. Call them.

Hannah considered the words she'd heard with every serving of meatloaf and mashed potatoes. "Your mom and dad love you, hon. Just call them."

Should she?

What if Allen was still there? What if nothing had changed?

For several minutes Hannah stood absolutely still, letting the snow cover her in large, soft flakes as she considered. Then she turned and walked toward the shelter and the phone.

If Allen answered, she'd hang up. If her mother

answered and Allen was still there, she'd hang up. One thing Carlos had taught her was that it's stupid to go back to what you ran away from in the first place.

She'd only go back if it was safe.

Dear reader,

We hope you enjoyed reading *Beyond the Crack in the Sidewalk*. Please take a moment to leave a review, even if it's a short one. Your opinion is important to us.

Discover more books by Maryann Miller at https://www.nextchapter.pub/authors/maryann-miller

Want to know when one of our books is free or discounted? Join the newsletter at http://eepurl.com/bqqB3H

Best regards,

Maryann Miller and the Next Chapter Team

ABOUT THE AUTHOR

Maryann Miller is an award-winning author of numerous books, screenplays, and stage plays. She started her professional career as a journalist, writing columns, feature stories, and short fiction for regional and national publications. A few of the awards Miller has received for her writing are the Page Edwards Short Story Award; the New York Library Best Books for Teens Award; first place in the short story and screenwriting contest at the Houston Writer's Conference; placing as a semi-finalist at Sundance; and placing as a semi-finalist in the Chesterfield Screenwriting Competition.

Stalking Season, the second book in her Seasons Mystery Series was chosen for the John E. Weaver Excellence in Reading award for Police Procedural Mysteries. *Doubletake,* was honored as the Best Mystery for 2015 by the Texas Association of Authors.

Previously published titles with Next Chapter

are: ***Evelyn Evolving***, ***One Small Victory*** and ***One Perfect Love.***

Miller can be found at her Amazon Author Page her Website on Twitter and Facebook and Goodreads

Lightning Source UK Ltd.
Milton Keynes UK
UKHW012141170921
390772UK00001B/116

9 781006 531644